·THE·
BUTTON
BOX

by MARGARETTE S. REID

illustrated by SARAH CHAMBERLAIN

A Puffin Unicorn

To my mother,
Anna Kerr Snyder,
who made beautiful things with her hands
M.S.R.

For Jamie
S.C.

PUFFIN UNICORN BOOKS
Published by the Penguin Group
Penguin Books USA Inc., 375 Hudson Street, New York, New York 10014, USA
Penguin Books Ltd, 27 Wrights Lane, London W8 5TZ, England
Penguin Books Australia Ltd, Ringwood, Victoria, Australia
Penguin Books Canada Ltd, 10 Alcorn Avenue, Toronto, Ontario, Canada M4V 3B2
Penguin Books (N.Z.) Ltd, 182-190 Wairau Road, Auckland 10, New Zealand
Penguin Books Ltd, Registered Offices: Harmondsworth, Middlesex, England

Text copyright © 1990 by Margarette S. Reid
Illustrations copyright © 1990 by Sarah Chamberlain
All rights reserved.
Unicorn is a registered trademark of Dutton Children's Books,
a division of Penguin Books USA Inc.
Library of Congress number 89-38566
ISBN 0-14-055495-5
Published in the United States by
Dutton Children's Books, a division of Penguin Books USA Inc.
Designed by Martha Rago
Printed in Hong Kong by South China Printing Company
First Puffin Unicorn Edition 1995
8 10 9 7

THE BUTTON BOX is also available in hardcover from Dutton Children's Books
and in a Spanish-language edition: LA CAJA DE LOS BOTONES.

My grandma has a special box.
I like to play with what's inside.

I swirl the buttons round and round, and then
I pick the ones I like.

Ten have flowers painted on them, just like Grandma's china dishes. I like to sort them first.

Next I look for sparkly buttons. I pretend they're jewels that once belonged to kings and queens and movie stars.

Some buttons are covered with cloth: satin, velvet, or corduroy. They make me think of fancy clothes.

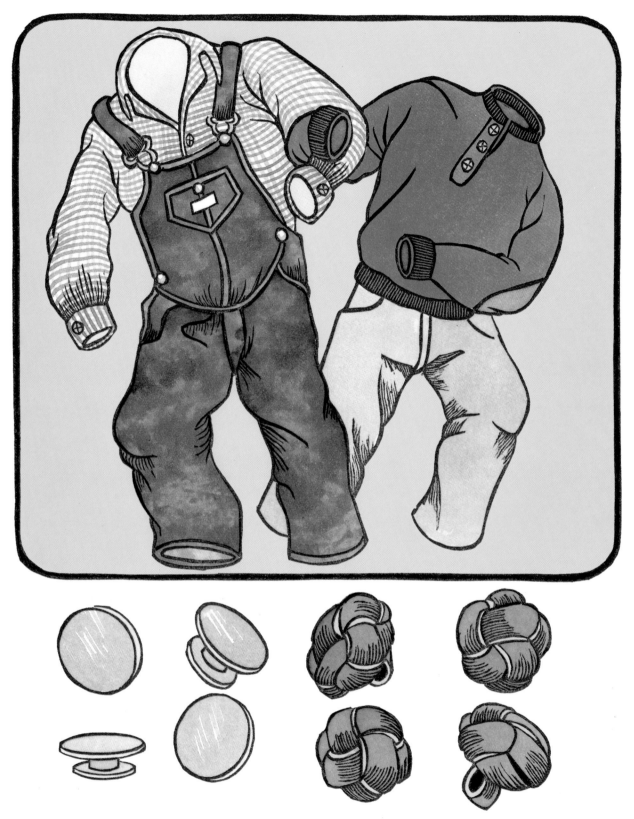

There are metal buttons from overalls and jeans, leather ones from cowboy shirts and sweaters.

This looks like one
from Grandpa's winter coat.

Grandma says these small ones came from shoes
worn long ago.

Next I sort the shiny buttons that come from uniforms.
I line them up like marchers in a big parade.

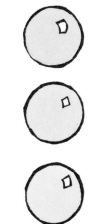

The one
with the
eagle I call
"Mr. President."

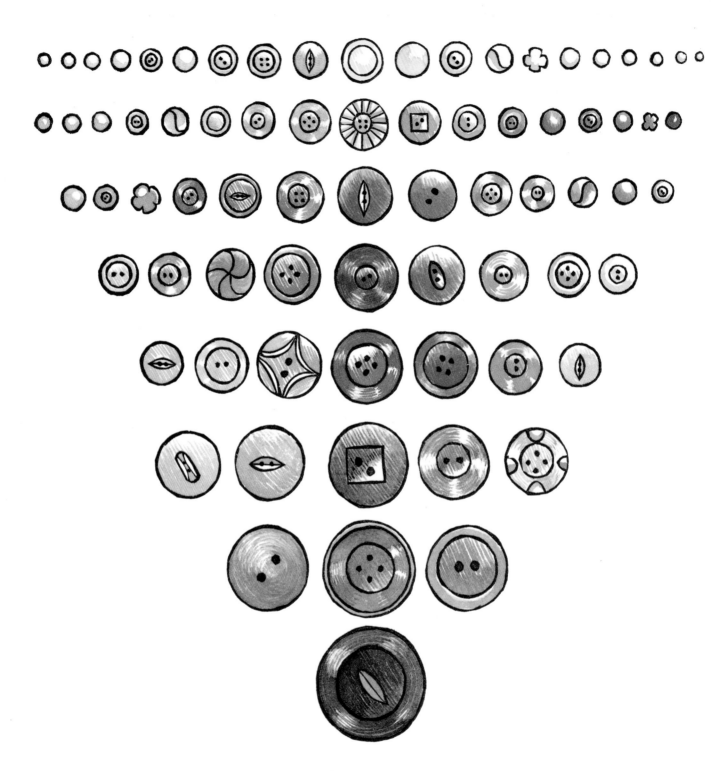

I pull out all the pearly ones and make a rainbow pattern. When does little change to big? I can never tell.

Some buttons have four holes, some two. Some don't have any sewing holes. They have shanks instead. These make good eyes on puppets or stuffed animals.

Sometimes when Grandma sorts with me, we play a special game. We stir the buttons, shut our eyes, and then we each take one. Grandma asks, "Are they alike?"

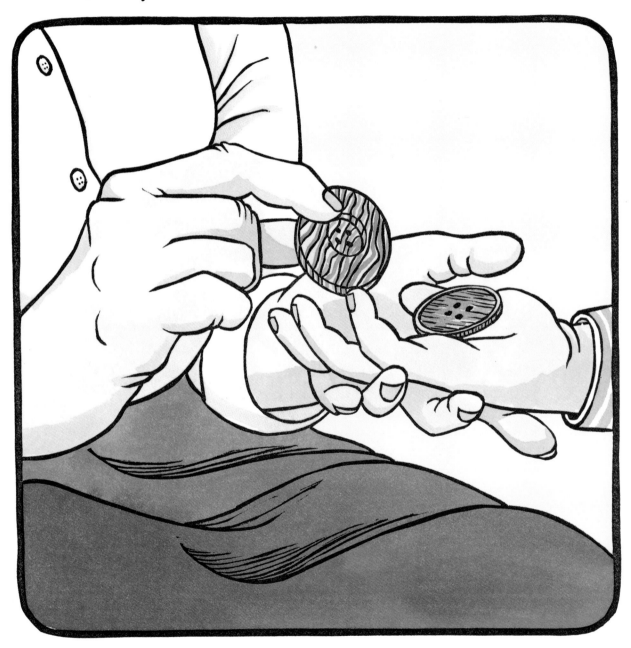

Mine is wooden. So is hers. Both are round and flat. But hers is thick and mine is thin.

She puts my button on a string. "Whirl it around,"
she says. The string twists up. I pull the ends.
We listen to it hum.

Grandma tells me what some buttons used to be. Some were seashells; some were even sand. Big furnaces heat the sand until it melts. When it cools, it's glass.

Wooden buttons come from trees.

Deer shed their antlers every winter and grow new ones in the spring. I like the buttons made from their old horns.

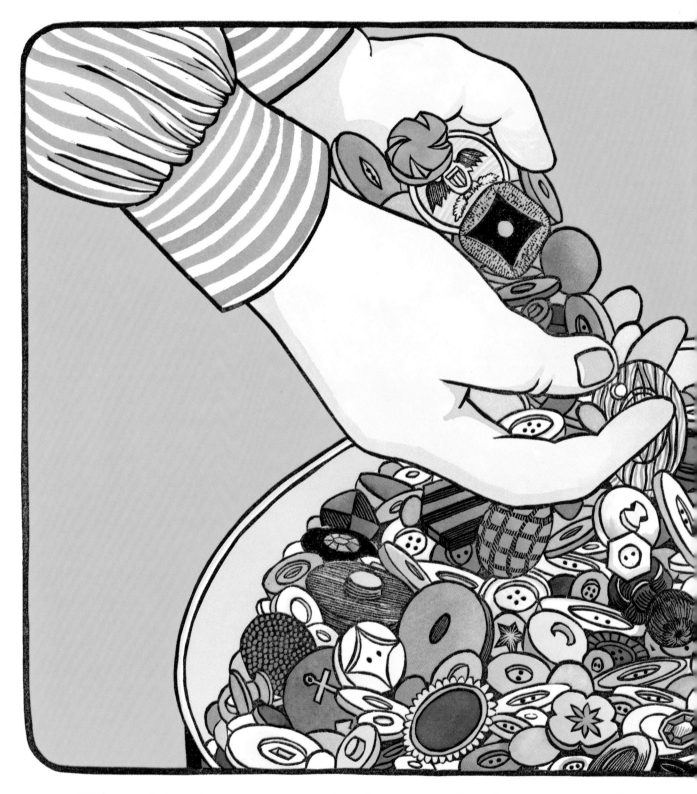

When it's time to put the buttons back, I pretend
I'm very rich, counting all my gold. I like to feel
the buttons then, the bumpy and the smooth.

I like the way they sound—clickety tappety—falling through my fingers, one by one, into the box.

Then Grandma puts the box away where it will wait till next time.

I wonder who first figured buttons out.

Buttons, Buttons, Who Invented Buttons?

No one knows who first figured buttons out. But when archeologists dig up towns and cities thousands of years old, they find pieces of stone, bone, clay, and metal that look like buttons.

For a long time, buttons were used with loops. Then, about eight hundred years ago, someone thought of fastening a piece of clothing by making a slit in it and slipping a button through. The buttonhole had been invented.

Around the thirteenth century, kings and courtiers began to wear buttons to show how rich and important they were. One French king had a suit covered with thirteen thousand, six hundred (13,600) buttons. Laws to keep ordinary people from wearing fancy buttons didn't last long.

Over the years, button makers carved, stamped, and molded buttons from ivory, pewter, glass, and a variety of other materials. Artists painted pictures of everything imaginable on buttons. Men wore buttons with pictures of their horses or dogs on them. Cut-steel buttons sparkled on ladies' gowns. Tiny pearl buttons decorated children's clothes.

During the American Revolution, patriots refused to buy English buttons, just as they refused to pay a tax on tea. Paul Revere, of the famous midnight ride, made fine silver buttons. Special buttons were designed for the inauguration of George Washington.

Although people still save buttons to use over and over, today many people collect them just for the fun of it.